MY SISTER IS SPECIAL

MY SISTER HAS DOWN SYNDROME

A Story About Acceptance

Marta Schmidt-Mendez, MA

DEDICATION

Over the years, I have had the privilege of working with many children diagnosed with Down syndrome. I could fill the pages of this book with their names and memories. This book is dedicated to Lois, one such child. Her parents were always so grateful for all I did for their daughter, never realizing that I received more than I gave. Lois did not survive her fourth birthday. Rest in peace little angel. You will always own a little piece of my heart and will always be remembered as the little girl who ran around blowing kisses and calling them "popos."

ACKNOWLEDGMENTS

Illustrations by: JJ Mendez

Olivia stood outside of the toy store, full of excitement. She and her mother were there to find her the perfect doll. Olivia was looking for a baby doll. This was going to be her very special baby doll. Olivia wanted a doll that looked just like a real baby. She wanted one that cried and could be fed. She also wanted to get things to go with her doll. She wanted a stroller, and diapers and one of those bottles that looked like the doll was really drinking. She wanted it all!!

Olivia's mother was having a baby in a few weeks. Olivia's mother had told her that the baby was going to be a girl and that now Olivia would be a big sister. Olivia was very excited. Olivia's mother had said that they could come to the store so that Olivia could pick out a special doll. Olivia was going to take care of her doll just like her mother and father were going to take care of her baby sister. Her parents had also said that Olivia would be able to help to take care of her baby sister. Olivia wanted to make sure that she had everything that she needed for her doll so that she could practice and be the best big sister ever! She had seen that her parents had bibs, bottles and little clothes. Olivia wanted the same things. Olivia could not wait to meet her baby sister. This was the most exciting thing that had ever happened in her life. She was very excited about her new role as a big sister.

Her friend Hannah, who lived in the same building, had a new baby sister. Olivia had noticed how exciting it was to bring the baby home. There had been a huge banner welcoming baby Michelle. People visited the family and everyone wanted to meet the baby. Everyone had cameras and took pictures. They brought presents for the baby, and for Hannah too. Everybody at Hannah's house was always smiling. If Hannah's mother or father was out in the hallway and somebody walked by, they smiled at them and congratulated them. The balloons and banners had been up for a very long time, even after the baby had come home. People always smiled when they walked by and saw them. Hannah's mother loved to show off the baby to anyone who would look. Olivia loved to go over to Hannah's house and loved spending time with the family. She could not wait until all of this happened at her house.

Olivia sat looking out of the window. She had her doll right next to her. Her mother and father had gone to the hospital that morning to have her baby sister. Olivia was at home with her aunt. Aunt Susie had asked Olivia if she wanted to watch a movie or to bake cookies. Olivia had said "no," and had remembered to add, "thank you," just like her parents had taught her to do. She had even turned down the chance to go to get ice cream, which was very unusual for her. Today, though, was an unusual day. Today was the day that Olivia officially became a big sister. Her father had said that after the baby was born and everyone was "settled," Olivia could go to visit her mother and her baby sister, who was going to be named Sarah. Olivia sat looking out of the window for what seemed to be a very long time. Finally, she saw her father's car and watched as he parked across the street.

Olivia was so excited. She started to jump up and down and ran to the door. As soon as her father walked in, she threw herself at him. "I'm ready, I'm ready," she squealed. "Not now Olivia," her father said without looking at her. "I am very tired right now, please get ready for bed," he said. "But Daddy, I want to go visit my baby sister and Mommy." "It's late Olivia, we can talk about it tomorrow."

Olivia was very sad and very confused. Her parents always kept their promise. She could not understand it and she cried a little as she put on her own pajamas and sat on her bed. It was early and she wasn't even sleepy. She suddenly got up, got her special baby doll, and put her in bed with her. She sat on her bed for a long time, thinking about her mother and her baby sister, until she finally fell asleep.

When Olivia got up the next morning, her father was already gone. Olivia's grandmother and Aunt Susie were sitting in the kitchen talking. As soon as Olivia walked in, they both stopped talking. Aunt Susie started to fuss over Olivia, asking her what she wanted for breakfast and trying to keep Olivia on one side of the kitchen. Olivia noticed that her grandmother had been crying. Olivia walked over to her grandmother. "Nana, when is Daddy coming to take me to see Mommy and Sarah?" Olivia asked. "Your mother and sister are coming home today Olivia," her grandmother answered. "When, when?" Olivia squealed. "I don't know when, now sit down and eat your breakfast," was all that her grandmother said. "Are we getting balloons?" Olivia asked hopefully. "No, Olivia, we are not getting balloons," said her grandmother sounding upset. "Please sit down and eat your breakfast and stop asking questions," her grandmother said as she turned away and walked out of the room. Olivia could not believe there would be no balloons. Olivia didn't think it was right not to have balloons. "Aunt Susie, when are we making the banner for my mother and my sister?" "We are not making one Olivia, so do as your grandmother said and sit down and eat your breakfast," was all that her aunt said. No balloons, no banner? What was going on? Why was everybody acting this way? This was very different than how Hannah's family reacted to Hannah's baby sister. Why couldn't her family be more like Hannah's? Olivia went to her room and sat in her little rocking chair cradling her special doll. Everybody was behaving so strangely. This is not what she had expected.

A few hours later, Olivia heard the front door open. Olivia ran from her room, "Mommy, Mommy, Mommy!! she shouted. Her mother hugged her. She looked sad. Her father walked in carrying something in a pink blanket. "Is that Sarah?" "Please, please, can I see her, can I see her?" asked Olivia. Her father bent down and opened the blanket and Olivia saw her sister for the first time. "Oh Mommy, she is so beautiful!" Olivia said. She looked up with a huge smile on her face only to see that both her mother and father were crying. "Why are you crying Mommy?" asked Olivia. "Don't you like Sarah?" Her mother didn't say anything, if anything, she just seemed to cry harder. Olivia felt so guilty. She looked at her father so see if he would do something, but he didn't. Her mother took Sarah from him and walked into the nursery they had waiting for her.

It was so strange. Nobody came to visit. Her Aunt Josie had called and her mother had spoken to her, but then her mother had started crying and had told her aunt that she would call her back another time. There were no balloons, no pictures, no presents. Olivia could not understand it. Each time that Olivia asked to help feed or change or even play with her baby sister, she was told that she couldn't and was told to go play with her special baby doll instead.

One day, Olivia went to the grocery store with her mother and Sarah. When they got home from the store, she walked into their building carrying a bag of groceries. Her mother was carrying Sarah. Mrs. James, one of the neighbors, was standing outside of her apartment, but as soon as she saw them coming, she quickly went inside and closed the door. Mrs. James always talked to everybody. Olivia's father always said that Mrs. James knew everybody's business. Today, though, she didn't even say hello. She didn't even ask to see Sarah, even though she always talked to Hannah's mother and always made funny sounds and faces at Hannah's baby sister.

The next day, Olivia and her mother went outside to get the mail. Olivia's mother was carrying Sarah. Just as they were getting to the mailbox, John, the mailman, was arriving. "Here you go," he said to her mother as he handed her a stack of mail. "Hello Olivia," he said to her and then hurried off. That's it. He never even looked at Sarah. John was always happy and he loved kids. Everyone always said that John was always late on his route because he stopped to talk to everyone and to play with the kids. Olivia wondered why nobody liked Sarah. Sarah was just a baby. What could Sarah have possibly done? How could people not like a baby? Olivia just did not understand. She was getting more and more confused every single day and just a little bit mad, too.

One day Olivia decided that it was not fair that she could not play with her sister, or that people did not visit and bring her and her sister presents. She went to her parents' room and knocked. Her mother told her to come in. Olivia's mother was sitting in the rocking chair with Sarah.

Olivia asked her mother one more time if she could play with her sister. "No Olivia, you can't," her mother said sadly. "Mommy, you said that as a big sister I could help if I listened to what you said." "Things are different now," her mother said. Olivia really couldn't understand what was different. She said, "Mommy, I have a sister and I don't get to do anything and it's not fair." Olivia was getting upset. "Olivia, many things aren't fair so please go to your room now," her mother answered. Olivia was really upset now. "No, I am tired of being told to go to my room whenever I ask to play with my sister." Olivia was near tears now. "Why can't I just be a big sister like everybody else?" she asked. Her mother looked at her and said, "You can't be a big sister like everybody else because your little sister is not like other babies. She has Down syndrome. Please Olivia, go to your room and play with your special baby doll," her mother said as she started to cry again.

Olivia walked to her room.

What was Down syndrome anyway?

So what if Sarah had Down syndrome or even Up syndrome?

Now Olivia was even more upset and more confused. She sat in her chair and looked at her doll. She did not like this baby doll. This doll did not have pretty eyes. Sarah's eyes were so pretty. Her eyes looked like her friend Emma's eyes. Emma's mother was from China. Olivia tried to move her doll's arms and legs but they did not move very much. Olivia had seen her mother and father changing her baby sister and her baby sister was very flexible. Her sister was flexible just like the gymnasts that Olivia had seen on television during the Olympics. Her doll was stiff. She sat in her chair and thought for a long, long time.

The next day Olivia was still upset and decided she had had enough of all of this.

She had to do something.

She took her doll and walked to her parents' room. Before knocking, she ran back into the kitchen and took her father's cell phone off of the charger where he kept it when he was home. She went back to her parents' room and knocked. She knocked very hard. She had things to say.

Her mother told her to come in. Her mother and father looked at her. They could tell she was upset. "What is it, Olivia?" her mother asked. "I want to be a big sister," Olivia demanded. "I want to take pictures of Sarah and I want to have balloons to celebrate," Olivia said. "I don't care about Down syndrome or whatever because I just care about my sister." "I care about Sarah, and so should everybody else." She continued, "I want people to visit us and to meet my sister." "I want people to be as happy as I am to have a baby sister."

Olivia walked over to her father and handed him her doll. "I don't want my doll because my doll is not special," Olivia announced.

"My sister is special, my sister has Down syndrome."

Olivia handed her father his phone and climbed on her mother's lap so that her mother could hold her too. "Smile Mommy, Daddy is going to take a picture of us girls," she said. Olivia stole a look at her mother just before her father snapped the picture. Her mother had tears in her eyes, but this time, she was also smiling.

ABOUT THE AUTHOR

Marta Schmidt-Mendez is a respected Child Development Specialist with over twenty-five years experience working with special needs children and their families.
Marta resides in Culver City, California with her husband, children, and dachshunds.